WORST MASCOT EVER

The Big idea Gang

WORST MASCOT EVER

James Preller
Illustrated by Stephen Gilpin

Houghton Mifflin Harcourt

BOSTON   NEW YORK

hmhco.com

The text was set in Adobe Caslon Pro.

Library of Congress Cataloging-in-Publication Data
Names: Preller, James, author. | Gilpin, Stephen, illustrator.
Title: Worst mascot ever / by James Preller ; illustrated by
Stephen Gilpin. Description: Boston ; New York : Houghton
Mifflin Harcourt, [2019] | Series: The Big Idea Gang |
Summary: Four friends inaugurate their Big Idea Gang by
starting a campaign to convince their principal and school
to get a new mascot. Identifiers: LCCN 2017061520 | ISBN
9781328857187 (hardback) | ISBN 9781328915115 (paperback)
Subjects: | CYAC: Mascots—Fiction. | Schools—Fiction. |
Persuasion (Psychology)—Fiction. | Friendship—Fiction. |
BISAC: JUVENILE FICTION / School & Education. |
JUVENILE FICTION / Humorous Stories. |
JUVENILE FICTION / Readers / Chapter Books. |
JUVENILE FICTION / Social Issues / Friendship.
Classification: LCC PZ7.P915 Wo 2018 | DDC [Fic]—dc23
LC record available at https://lccn.loc.gov/2017061520

Printed in the United States of America
DOC 10 9 8 7 6 5 4 3 2 1
4500739483

This book is dedicated to Mr. Met.

—J. P.

Table of Contents

Chapter 1 Armadillo Blues   1

Chapter 2 Lizzy's Terrific, Amazing, Stupendous, Fabulous Idea . . . Almost!   8

Chapter 3 Zombie Eyeballs   16

Chapter 4 "Wow Me"   22

Chapter 5 Problem on the Playground   28

Chapter 6 At the Library   34

Chapter 7 Meeting with the Big Boss   41

Chapter 8 Suri Leads the Revolt   48

Chapter 9 The Campaign   54

Chapter 10 Lizzy Gets a Little Help   61

Chapter 11 Imagine   68

Chapter 12 Enter the Dragon   79

Miss Zips's "Wow Me" Tips   83

— CHAPTER 1 —

Armadillo Blues

The trouble began when a giant purple armadillo ran onto the field behind Clay Elementary School.

Well, "ran" isn't exactly the right word.

No, not "jogged" either.

The armadillo stumbled.

It bumbled.

It huffed and puffed.

It gasped.

And finally paused, panting, to face a gathered crowd of students. The armadillo bellowed into a megaphone, "ARE YOU READY—FOR —*gasp, wheeze*—THE FUN RUN?"

Pointing his right front claw, the armadillo led the charge. He ran forward, but his tail snagged on a tree root. *Rip! Whoops!* No more tail! Cotton stuffing floated into the air, carried by the wind.

Shivering in the cold November afternoon, students of Clay Elementary watched in wonder. They stood huddled together like a colony of penguins. The boys and girls were not dressed for the chilly weather. Most wore running shorts, T-shirts, and sneakers. A few pulled on wool hats and gloves. It was time for the annual Fun Run for Fitness.

"I'm freezing!" Connor O'Malley complained.

His teeth chattered. "I can't feel my toes." He turned to his twin sister, Lizzy. "Are my lips turning blue? I actually think my face has frozen solid. I might freeze to death."

Lizzy poked her brother's cheek with a finger. "It feels like a hockey puck." She grinned. "I think you'll survive."

"Hey, why aren't you cold?" Connor asked.

"I came prepared. I stuffed heat packs into my socks," Lizzy said. "Just call me Toasty Toes."

"Oh no!" Kym Park interjected. "Look now."

All eyes turned to watch as the school's purple mascot, Arnold the Armadillo, slipped and tripped and sprawled belly-first into an icy mud puddle.

"Whoa, belly flop," Connor said.

"Ladies and gentlemen, the armadillo has landed," Deon Gibson observed.

Connor and Deon bumped fists.

Every student at Clay Elementary knew that Principal Tuxbury was in there. Deon shook his head. "Worst . . . mascot . . . ever."

Lizzy frowned. "The costume does seem a little droopy."

"I'll say," Connor agreed.

"It's a sad, sorry armadillo," Deon added.

"I wonder why we have an armadillo for a mascot," Lizzy mused. "We live in Connecticut. I don't think there are any armadillos in Connecticut. Are there?"

"We have possums," Deon said. "That's kind of the same. Isn't it?"

Lizzy frowned.

Kym had other concerns. "I hope Principal Tuxbury isn't hurt." She was right to fret. Groans echoed from inside the armadillo's plush-and-chicken-wire head. Ms. Baez, the school nurse, rushed to the fallen mascot. She began yanking on the armadillo's head.

"It's stuck. Nurse Baez needs help," Kym said.

"Let's go!" Connor roared.

In moments, students and teachers formed a long chain—all yanking and tugging on the fallen armadillo's head.

"Oof, huzzuh, gork!" Muffled cries came from inside the mascot.

The head remained fixed to the body of the costume. It would not budge. Principal Tuxbury was trapped.

"Should we call the fire department?" Kym asked. No one replied to Kym's question. Because no one heard it. The screaming was too loud.

"Heave!" beseeched Nurse Baez.

"Ho!" the students cried.

"HEAVE!"

"HO!"

And finally, with one mighty tug, the head ripped off. It flew up into the sky. The long line of tuggers toppled to the ground, heels kicking the air.

The grubby mascot sat up. The headless costume now exposed the bald, round, unhappy head

of Principal Larry Tuxbury. He looked around, dazed and confused.

"Are you all right, Mr. Tuxbury?" Nurse Baez asked. "Perhaps you should lie down on a cot."

"Never again," he muttered. "You'll never, ever get me into that ridiculous suit again!"

From that day forward, it would always be remembered as the best Fun Run ever.

It was the day the armadillo died.

CHAPTER 2

Lizzy's Terrific, Amazing, Stupendous, Fabulous Idea . . . Almost!

The next morning students trickled into room 312. They hung up their jackets. They pulled homework folders from their backpacks. They stuffed lunch boxes in their cubbies. It was a mellow time of day, full of yawns and quiet conversation. The room was arranged in four-desk clusters, called tables. At that time of day, students were free to move around as they wished

—until Principal Tuxbury's morning announcements.

The boys and girls called their teacher "Miss Zips." That's because her name was Isadora Zipsokowski, a name few managed to pronounce without spraining their tongues. Miss Zips was six feet tall in flat shoes. She usually wore her hair in a tight, black bun. There were often pencils sticking out of it. Miss Zips had the whitest, straightest teeth anyone had ever seen. All the kids agreed she could be an actress for a toothpaste commercial.

Miss Zips was crazy about reading. Her classroom was filled with books—in stacks, on shelves, in bins, and jammed into boxes labeled WINTER! or HALLOWEEN! or GRAPHIC NOVELS! and so on.

Once a student named Bartimus Finkle complained, "Our room is a mess. Too many books."

Miss Zips's eyes narrowed. She replied, "Better get used to it, Bartimus. Books are my favorite furniture."

On this morning, Miss Zipsokowski sat at her desk nibbling a blueberry muffin. She chatted with Mr. Sanders, the classroom aide. He was famous for his big, gray, bushy eyebrows. Deon had quipped, "It's like he has a squirrel's tail stapled above each eyelid."

Lizzy and Kym visited with Connor and Deon, who sat at the same table.

"Kym and I have a great, amazing idea," Lizzy

announced. She wore stretch pants, a green fleece, and slip-on glitter shoes.

"Uh-oh," Connor groaned. He turned to Deon. "You know what happened last time Lizzy had an idea?"

"What?" Deon asked.

"More homework!" Connor replied.

"Not true!" Lizzy protested.

"Is true," Connor answered.

"Not!" Lizzy said.

"It is true," Connor confided to Deon. "Last year, Lizzy actually suggested that our teacher give us homework on weekends."

"I didn't want *more* homework," Lizzy said. "I just thought he could spread it out more evenly."

"Like a peanut butter sandwich," Connor said, rolling his eyes.

"Exactly," Lizzy said. "Nobody wants the peanut butter in clumps and lumps. It's the same with homework!"

This debate went on for a few minutes. The twins batted the words "is" and "not" back and forth like shuttlecocks over a badminton net. Their voices grew louder. Finally Deon groaned, "Guys, you've gotta stop. My ears are bleeding."

Kym said in a soft voice, "We never got to tell you our idea."

Deon opened his mouth. But before he could protest, Miss Zips was at his elbow. "What's going on, guys?"

"We were trying to tell them our terrific, amazing, stupendous idea," Lizzy said.

"So why the raised voices?" Miss Zips looked to Connor and Deon.

Connor didn't answer. He stared at his desktop.

Deon fiddled with a pencil.

Miss Zips turned to Lizzy and Kym. "I can't speak for the boys. But I'm excited to hear your terrific, amazing, stupendous idea."

"We want a new school mascot," Kym and Lizzy announced.

"Oh," Miss Zips said. "You don't like Arnold the Armadillo?"

"No," Kym said.

"Not even a little bit," Lizzy added.

"It's the worst," Deon agreed.

Miss Zips glanced at the wall clock. "So what's your idea for a new mascot?"

"Our idea?" Lizzy echoed.

Her ears began to twitch.

"Yes. You've made your claim, now you need to support it. What did you have in mind? And also, who would you need to convince in order to make this change happen?" Miss Zips wondered.

Lizzy looked at Kym.

Kym looked at Connor.

Connor looked at Deon.

For the next half a minute, everyone's head spun around like a weather vane on a windy day. Round and round they went. Kym finally admitted, "We don't have a clue."

"Hmm," Miss Zips replied. "You've got some thinking to do. I'd start by focusing on the new mascot."

"Good morning, Clay Elementary!" a voice blared over the loudspeaker. Mouths zipped shut. It was time to stand, hand to heart, and face the flag.

CHAPTER 3

Zombie Eyeballs

After school, Lizzy, Connor, and Kym met at Deon's house. They agreed that his house was the best choice, because it had the yummiest snacks. Mr. Gibson was a photographer who often traveled for business. Mrs. Gibson worked from home. Nobody knew exactly what she did. It seemed to involve a lot of sighing and tapping on the computer keyboard.

"Probably a writer," Connor speculated. "Writers sigh a lot."

In the basement, the four friends munched on grapes, Pop-Tarts, and goldfish. "Miss Zips is right," Kym said. "We need a big idea."

"We already have one. We're going to dump

Arnold the Armadillo," Deon said, rubbing his hands together. "My work is done here."

Lizzy shook her head. "Not so fast, Deon. How do we do it? We're not in charge of the school."

"I wish," Connor said. "If I were boss, I'd ban homework forever. And Wednesdays."

"Wednesdays? The whole day?" Kym asked.

"Wednesday are terrible," Connor said. "Trust me. Nothing good ever happened on a Wednesday."

"Nice dream, Connor," Lizzy said. "But I think we should start by coming up with a cool new mascot. Has anyone got any ideas?"

Kym suggested that maybe the mascot should be named after the state animal. They looked it up on the home computer.

Connor read over Kym's shoulder, "A sperm whale?"

The gang decided that "Let's go, Sperm Whales!" wasn't very catchy.

"What about the state bird?" Lizzy asked.

"It's the robin," Kym said.

"Boring!" Deon pronounced.

"What about the state fish?" Connor asked.

Kym rolled her eyes. "It's the shad."

"Nope, not on my watch," Deon piped up. "No way. We are not going to be the Clay Elementary Shad. I'm sorry, that's just not happening."

Everyone laughed. The shad was nobody's idea of a great school mascot.

Deon was growing bored. He hated to be trapped indoors on a sunny day. He popped a grape into his mouth and snapped down on it. "I like to pretend they're zombie eyeballs," he explained to Connor, who understood perfectly.

"That's an idea for our mascot," Connor exclaimed. "Zombies!" He wandered around the room on stiff legs, moaning and groaning.

"Gross." Lizzy frowned.

Kym twisted around in her chair. In a soft voice she offered, "Everybody likes hamsters. What do you guys think?"

Deon hissed and gave two thumbs down.

"I don't hear any ideas coming from you, Deon," Kym snapped.

"The Bulldogs," Deon replied.

There was a long pause.

No one said a word.

"Bulldogs *are* cute," Lizzy finally said.

"I like their pushed-in faces," Kym said.

"And they're tough," Connor added.

"The Clay Elementary Bulldogs," Kym murmured, nodding her head. "Deon, I think you've done it."

19

"Genius," Connor agreed, rising to his feet. "Now let's go outside. I'm tired of eating zombie eyeballs. Besides, I saw a big pile of leaves on the front lawn. Let's jump in 'em."

"What about ticks?" Kym worried.

"For a mascot?" Deon asked.

Kym rolled her eyes. "No, ticks in the leaves! They carry diseases." But Connor was already halfway up the stairs. He wasn't listening, and he wasn't the worrying type.

CHAPTER 4

"Wow Me"

Lizzy decided that morning snack was the perfect time to ask Miss Zips for help. Boys and girls ate at their desks. But afterward, they could roam around, practice dance routines on the rug, pull out a book, get a head start on homework, talk quietly, whatever.

"Notebooks away," Miss Zips announced. "Get ready for snack."

All at once, the activity in the room shifted. Everybody got busy eating crackers, applesauce, cookies, cheese puffs, pretzel sticks, carrots, potato chips, and strawberries.

Mr. Sanders went over to help organize Bobby Mumford, who was humming to himself while carelessly dropping Cheetos on the rug.

"Now's our chance," Lizzy said, elbowing Kym.

They told Miss Zips that her sweater was a pretty color. Then they told her about their idea for a bulldog mascot. Then Lizzy asked, "What do we do now?"

Miss Zips thought for a moment. "You'll surely need to speak to Principal Tuxbury. You should make an appointment with the secretary, Ms. Woon."

"Can you do it for us?" Lizzy asked.

Miss Zips didn't say yes right away. Not a good sign. "You know what?" she said. "I think it might be more helpful . . . if I make you do it yourselves."

"But we're just kids," Kym said.

Miss Zips waved away the thought. "Oh, don't be silly. You've got a big idea. Now you've got to sell it. Remember, you have to support your claim."

Lizzy and Kym sagged. They didn't know the first thing about selling ideas. The phone rang and Miss Zips went to answer it. Before picking up the receiver, she said to the girls, "Let me think about this. I won't leave you high and dry."

"What does that mean?" Lizzy asked Kym.

"It means there's hope," Kym said.

Ten minutes later, Miss Zips signaled the end of snack break. She slid her fancy black chair with roller wheels to the front of the room. "Come, gather round," she said. "Bring your clipboards." Miss Zips loved to teach with her students huddled together on the reading rug.

The students all had their own clipboards. This way they could take notes while sitting crisscross-applesauce. She said, "Be thoughtful about who you sit with. Are we all settled? That's good." She rested her hands in her lap. "Ah, that was a nice little break, wasn't it? I was speaking to Lizzy and Kym earlier today, and they have a really big idea." She looked to Lizzy. "Would you like to tell the class about it?"

Lizzy explained their big idea.

It was time for a new school mascot.

The bulldog!

The kids in room 312 were thrilled. "I never liked that armadillo," confided Amir Kazemi.

"Why not?" asked Rosa Morales.

"He once stepped on my foot. It really hurt," Amir said, remembering the pain.

Bobby Mumford raised his hand. In a flat voice he informed the class, "My cousin Earl has a friend and his uncle has a bulldog named Buzzy."

"Ah, well, thank you for sharing that, Bobby,"

Miss Zips replied. "I've told Lizzy and Kym that they will have to present their idea to Principal Tuxbury."

Lizzy nodded, not sure if she was up for the task.

"You are going to have to really wow him," Miss Zips said.

That was Miss Zips's favorite expression. *Wow me.* She reminded the class, "That means, knock

his socks off! Give it your best effort. I want you to astonish him. I want Principal Tuxbury to feel bedazzled, flabbergasted, stupefied, astounded, thunderstruck, and amazed—all at the same time."

"That sounds exhausting," Deon said, collapsing onto Connor's shoulder.

While everyone laughed at Deon's antics, one voice spoke up.

"If you ask me, it's a *terrible* idea," the voice said. All eyes turned to look at Suri Brewster, sitting in the back row. She sat with her arms folded across her chest, mouth tight, like she was sucking on a lemon.

"Thank you for speaking up," Miss Zips said. "What are your objections, Suri?"

"Arnold has always been the school mascot. There's no reason to change now." Suri glared across the rug at Lizzy. "Everybody loves Arnold."

Uh-oh, thought Lizzy. *Trouble.*

No one in room 312 dared cross Suri Brewster.

— CHAPTER 5 —

Problem on the Playground

Suri Brewster was small and wiry, with thick black hair and pointy glasses with purple rims. She had a way of leaning forward when she walked as if pushing against a strong wind, fists clenched. No one had named Suri the boss of the playground, the queen of room 312, or even the master of the universe. It only seemed that way. Suri naturally took charge.

Of everything and everybody.

During recess, she spied Lizzy and Kym by the climbing wall. Suri said "Harumph!" and marched over. Two other kids—Otis Smick and Rosa Morales—followed close behind.

"We don't like what you're trying to do," Suri said. She stood with her feet apart, hands on her hips, a scowl on her face. The scowl wasn't new. She was born with it. Suri often looked as if there was something sour in her mouth—a bad taste that pushed her lips outward.

"Oh?" Lizzy said.

"We don't want a new school mascot," Suri said. "There's nothing wrong with Arnold the Armadillo."

"Well, we were thinking—" Kym began.

"Everybody loves Arnold," Suri stated.

"Not everybody," Kym offered, in a faltering voice.

Suri crossed her arms. She glared at Kym.

"There's nothing the matter with Arnold. Besides, we can't be the Bulldogs. That's from the University of Georgia. My father went there and I know."

Otis Smick chortled.

Rosa beamed.

Kym didn't know what to say.

She hadn't heard about the Georgia Bulldogs before.

But Lizzy said, "The truth is, we haven't decided yet."

"Harumph." Suri kicked at the dirt with the heel of her shoe. "I think Arnold is just fine. I don't like change. Nobody does. It's better when things stay the same. Arnold today, Arnold forever."

"I'm somebody," Kym finally said, her voice stronger. "There's a lot of somebodies around here. You're not the boss of us."

Suri's eyes blazed. The corner of her lip curled into a sneer. "I'll fight this every step of the way," she said. And then she turned to Otis and Rosa. "Let's make like a tree and leave."

Otis stood rooted to the ground, confused.

"Come on, Otis," Rosa said.

A minute later, Connor and Deon joined the girls. "Whoa, what was that all about?" Connor asked.

"Trouble," Kym uttered.

Deon watched as Suri climbed the monkey bars. "She's a little scary," he admitted.

Lizzy nodded. "This isn't going to be easy after all. But we can't let her stop us. We have homework to do."

"Homework?" bleated Deon.

"We're going to hit the library," Lizzy said. "We have to think up a new mascot. Personally, I think bulldogs are too slobbery."

"Suri doesn't agree with us," Kym said. "We have to come up with reasons to help change her mind."

Deon mused, "This reminds me of my birthday last year."

Kym blinked.

Lizzy said, "What?"

Deon smiled. "I had to talk my parents into getting me a fat-tire bike for my birthday. It wasn't easy. They said I was too young. They said I wouldn't take care of it. They said it was too expensive."

"Oh, I get it," Lizzy said. "You had to come up with good reasons."

"So what did you do?" Connor asked.

Deon's eyes twinkled. "What I always do—I begged."

"Classy," Kym muttered.

— CHAPTER 6 —

At the Library

That afternoon, Lizzy, Kym, Connor, and Deon met at the town library. They sat around a horse-shoe-shaped couch, before a small coffee table stacked with books. Deon suggested they should call themselves the WOW Kids in honor of Miss Zips.

"Say what?" Connor said.

Deon explained that WOW was an acronym. It was short for "Writing Our Wish."

Deon looked at the others. "Catchy, huh?"

"Sure," Connor said, flopping back on the couch. "Like the flu."

"What about the BIG?" Kym said. "The Big Idea Gang? I bet Miss Zips would like it."

"Not bad," Deon said.

"Not bad is pretty good," Connor clucked.

They got down to business.

"Remember what Miss Zips told us," Lizzy said. "If we want to persuade people, like Suri or Principal Tuxbury, we're going to need support. Facts. Not just opinions."

Connor flipped through the pages of a book.

Kym opened a laptop.

Lizzy opened her notebook.

And Deon . . . just sort of chilled.

"You have to admit it, armadillos are cool," Connor said.

Kym read from the *National Geographic* website. "Armadillo is a Spanish word meaning 'little armored one.'"

Deon leaned forward, interested.

Kym said, "There are lots of different kinds. They like warm weather. Most armadillos live in South America."

She frowned, searched for a different site. "The nine-banded armadillo has made its way into the southern United States," she read.

"Not Connecticut," Deon said, though he wasn't exactly sure.

Kym scanned the laptop screen. "They've been found as far north as Missouri. But I don't think there's ever been an armadillo in Connecticut."

"See what I've been saying!" Lizzy exclaimed. "We can use these facts in our presentation."

"I could draw a map," Deon offered. "I've got

mad coloring skills." He blew on his fingernails and rubbed them against his chest.

"Gross," Kim said, eyes glued to the computer screen. "They eat bugs. Worms, maggots, snails, beetles."

"Doesn't bother me," Deon said. "I'm still hungry. Seriously. Have you guys got any money? Maybe we could get some pizza?"

"No pizza, Deon. We have work to do. Food is all you ever think about," Kym said.

Deon shrugged. "Sometimes I sleep."

Kym laughed.

Connor had an idea. "You know what we need?"

No one knew what they needed.

Finally, Lizzy took the bait. "Okay, I give. What do we need, Connor?"

"A chart."

"A chart?"

"Yeah, a chart. Like in that book the Zipster read to us yesterday," Connor said.

"She's the Zipster now?" Kym asked, eyebrows raised.

Connor shrugged. "What was the name of that book? About the girl who wants a pet giraffe?"

"*One Word from Sophia*," Kym answered.

"That's it!" Connor snapped his fingers. "Sophia knew how to persuade her parents. She didn't give up. She made a graph. And, and—"

"—and she didn't give up," Kym said.

"Awesome, we'll make a pie chart!" Connor exclaimed.

"You guys are making me hungry with all this talk about pie," Deon muttered. "Has anybody got anything to eat?"

Lizzy reached into her backpack. She tossed a baggie of pretzel nuggets to Deon. She said to Connor, "Suri was right about the Bulldogs. They are the mascot for Georgia football. Not to mention the slime factor. Have you got any other ideas?"

"Hey, I still like the zombies," Deon suggested.

Kym shook her head. "Get real, Deon. Principal Tuxbury would never let us."

"Kym's right. It would never fly," Lizzy agreed.

Connor glanced at the window. The wind blustered. People hurried in and out of the library's front doors. There was an old man dragging a wagon filled with books up the walkway.

Dragging a wagon?

Dragon a wagon?

Get real? Never fly?

Hmm.

"What about . . . dragons?" Connor offered. "You know, the imaginary creatures. They fly around and shoot fire out of their mouths."

"We know what dragons are," Lizzy said.

"Yeah we do, and they're awesome!" Deon exclaimed. "I love it. What do you think, Kym?"

"A fire-breathing dragon would look hot on a T-shirt," she conceded. "Dragons are really popular right now."

"Good, it's settled," Lizzy stated. "We'll go

for the Clay Elementary Dragons. Beats an armadillo any day. All agreed?"

"Totally," Deon said, slapping his hands together. "Now can we eat? Because I'm still seriously starving."

— CHAPTER 7 —

Meeting with the Big Boss

The gang knew it was time to talk to Principal Tuxbury. Deon and Connor went to their teacher for advice. They told Miss Zips the plan. "Goodbye Arnold, hello dragon!" Deon explained.

Connor asked, "But how do we convince Principal Tuxbury? Do you have any secret tips, Miss Zips?"

Miss Zips smiled. "There's no magic key, just hard work. If you can support your claim, he's sure to listen. But first you'll have to make an appointment to see him."

"An appointment? Like at the dentist?" Deon asked.

Connor gulped. He did not have happy memories of the dentist. He imagined five fat fingers fumbling inside his mouth. He could almost hear the high-pitched whirr of a drill.

His face turned pale.

His gums hurt just thinking about it.

"I think it will be less painful than the dentist," Miss Zips said, resting a hand on Connor's shoulder.

"I hope so," Connor mumbled.

"Now remember," Miss Zips said. "When you want to persuade someone to do something, you

make a claim and offer support. So you want a new mascot—why should anyone listen to you? What are your reasons? Then you must anticipate his objections."

Deon's eyes shot blanks.

"Anticipate objections?" Connor echoed.

Miss Zips smiled. "Think of it this way. Imagine that you want to go to the park, but your friend wants to stay home and watch TV. You have to try to get inside his brain. Ask yourself, 'Why doesn't he want to go to the park with me?' Think of his possible reasons, or objections. It's too far? It might rain? He has homework to do?"

"Oh, I get it," Deon said. "I'd be like, dude, it's beautiful out, we'll go for a couple of hours, everybody will be there, and nobody cares about homework anyway!"

"What?!" Miss Zips's eyes grew large.

"Just joking," Deon said. "I'd tell him that there will still be plenty of time to do homework after dinner."

Miss Zips nodded. "Good, I think you've got

the hang of it. In the art of persuasion, you have to—"

"—anticipate objections!" Deon and Connor said in unison.

Miss Zips smiled. "Yes, you have to think about what his opposing claims might be and give him reasons to change his mind."

"Whatever you say, Miss Zips," Connor said. "Do you want to come with us? You could do all the talking!"

"Sorry, boys. You're on your own," Miss Zips said.

"That's okay," Deon spoke up. "We'll get Lizzy to do it."

* * *

The next afternoon, Lizzy and Kym sat in Principal Tuxbury's office. The tips of their feet barely reached the floor. Deon and Connor stood behind them. They held a poster that showed the habitat of armadillos. It was a map of South

America and North America. At the top, in bold letters, it read:

ZERO ARMADILLOS IN CONNECTICUT
NONE, ZIPPO, ZILCH, NADA!

Lizzy handled the explaining.

Principal Tuxbury sat in a brown, high-backed chair behind a big, cluttered desk. He listened, rubbed his chin, and murmured comments such as "Hmm" or "Ah, I see."

Finally he leaned forward. He stared at the girls for a long minute without speaking. "So that's what this is about? You want the school to go out and buy a new mascot? Is that it?"

Lizzy turned to Kym. Her stomach gurgled. "Well, not exactly . . . ," she stammered. Something in his tone worried Lizzy. Doubt shook her confidence.

"Yes," Kym spoke up. "And it's not just us. A lot of students think it's time for new ideas."

Connor and Deon nodded encouragingly.

"Besides, the armadillo costume is ruined anyway," Kym continued. "Now's our chance to try something new."

"And," Connor spoke up, "you would never have to dress up as an armadillo again."

"Hmmmm," murmured Principal Tuxbury.

There was a gleam of light in his eye.

CHAPTER 8

Suri Leads the Revolt

A flicker of a smile flashed across Principal Tux-bury's face. He shut his eyes, as if imagining him-self never—ever, ever—wearing that hot, smelly costume again.

"You make some good points," he mused. "You're right about one thing. We will have to purchase a new costume, regardless. The old one is already in the Dumpster. So what's your idea for a new mascot?"

On cue, Deon dramatically tossed the old poster to the floor. Connor held up a new poster showing a drawing of a dragon. They had gotten the best artist in the school, Padma Bitar, to do it.

And it looked amazing.

"Meet Drake the Dragon," Connor announced. "Pretty fierce, huh? Soon we'll be known far and wide as the Clay Elementary Dragons!"

"No one will ever mess with us again!" Deon added.

Principal Tuxbury nodded. He pulled thoughtfully on his lower lip. "Very nice job, kids. You might be correct. Maybe it is time for a change," Principal Tuxbury decided.

Noises started up in the hallway. Principal Tuxbury tilted his head. He listened. Voices argued outside his door.

"I can't let you in," his secretary said. "He's in a meeting."

"We demand our rights!" a girl's voice exclaimed.

Kym looked at Lizzy. They knew the person who was attached to that voice. It could only be Suri Brewster—and she sounded furious. Meanwhile, the hallway noises got louder. Students were chanting in protest, "Arnold today! Arnold forever!"

Principal Tuxbury rose. He walked to the door, pulled it open, and stuck his head outside.

"We demand our rights!" Suri erupted. "Arnold the Armadillo has been the mascot for Clay Elementary for over sixty years!" she announced. "It's tradition!"

"Calm down, Suri," Principal Tuxbury said in soothing tones. "Please lower your voice. Come into my office and we'll talk about it."

In a moment Principal Tuxbury was back at his desk. Suri stood in front of it, talking a mile a minute. Principal Tuxbury frowned. It was as if a dark cloud had settled down over his head and now it had begun to rain. Once again, he murmured comments such as "Hmm" or "Ah, I see."

It appeared Principal Tuxbury might be changing his mind. "Uh-oh," Lizzy whispered to her brother.

"Are you finished?" the principal asked Suri.

"Yes, sir," she said.

He looked at all five children gathered in the room. There was a sparkle to his eyes—a glint of pride. "Tell you what we'll do," he said. "We'll have a school-wide election. The students can vote if they want to keep Arnold . . . or go with the dragon. Dudley, Daryl, Dougie, or—"

"Drake," Connor corrected. "Drake the Dragon."

"Ah, yes," Principal Tuxbury said. "Drake."

Lizzy exchanged glances with Kym, Connor,

and Deon. She silently agreed with the principal. "We think an election would be good for school spirit," she said.

Kym leaped to her feet. "A vote would be the American way!" She gestured to the flag in the corner of the room.

"It would be exciting!" Connor added, also rising.

Deon begun to hum the song "America." *My country 'tis of thee . . .*

Suri scowled, unsure what to think. She had wanted Arnold the Armadillo, not a democracy.

"Yes, yes, an election—we'll let the students decide," Principal Tuxbury said. "I'll speak with Miss Zipsokowski. So long as this doesn't take away too much from class time, I can't see the harm of it."

"Oh, thank you!" Lizzy and Kym exclaimed.

Connor and Deon cheered.

The principal turned to Suri. "Does that sound fair to you? I don't want to trample on any-one's rights."

Suri nodded without smiling. She had won the battle, but not the war. Outside in the hallway, a chorus of five voices continued to chant, "Arnold today! Arnold forever!"

"Are those friends of yours?" Principal Tuxbury asked Suri.

She said they were. "I asked them to come."

"Good," he replied, rubbing his eyes. "You've made your point. Now could you please ask them to go away? It's been a long day."

CHAPTER 9

The Campaign

Across the school, the election made big news.

On Monday morning, Rosa Morales and thick-necked Otis Smick stood at the front doors. They handed out flyers and greeted incoming students with the words "Vote for Arnold!"

Lizzy folded her arms and refused to take a flyer. Instead she smiled tightly and said, "No thanks. Save a tree."

In the main lobby, Suri was hanging a large wall poster. It looked terrific, with big, fat letters and a photo of an armadillo on the right side. Students lingered admiringly. The excitement over the big vote was building.

Lizzy and Connor stopped to read it.

A.A.A.A.
Armadillos
Are
Actually
Awesome!

VOTE FOR ARNOLD!

When Suri noticed her rivals gaping at the poster, she smirked. "Oh, hi, Lizzy. Hi, Connor. I hope you don't mind that I took the best spot. Your team doesn't seem to have any posters yet anyway, do you?"

Lizzy grumbled a low growl, like a cornered animal. When she turned to leave, Suri called out, "Remember, the election is only three days away!"

"She's pretty serious about this," Connor said.

Lizzy stormed down the hall, feet clomping noisily. Cheeks red, teeth gritted. She stopped suddenly to stare at a flyer taped to the wall. It showed a photo of Arnold from last year's assembly. The giant plush armadillo stood on the stage with both arms raised in triumph. Underneath it read EVERYBODY LOVES ARNOLD!

"*Grrrrr*," Lizzy growled.

Once inside the classroom, Lizzy flung her backpack into the cubby. *Whomp, thump, crash.* She plopped into her chair.

Kym sat across from her at the table, afraid to speak.

Finally Lizzy said, "My house. After school. Tell the gang."

Kym smiled to herself. "Good," she said.

"And tell them to bring art supplies," Lizzy said. "We've got work to do."

"I'll say. But we'll need more than art projects to win the election," Kym said. "We have to get ready for the big assembly on Thursday morning. Somebody has to give a speech in front of the entire school."

At Connor and Lizzy's house, the gang sat around a large dining room table. It was strewn with white posterboard, crayons, markers, scissors, glitter, and puddles of glue.

Padma Bitar had joined them. Padma was busy drawing different pictures of Drake the Dragon on the posters. A billow of fire came from his mouth. "That's lit," Deon said approvingly. "You are killin' it, Padma."

Padma looked up at Deon. "Seriously? You like it?"

"Yeah, I do," Deon said. "But can you draw it, like, I don't know, with the fire *cooking* an armadillo?"

"That would be so great," Connor said.

"No," Kym interrupted. "That would be sooooo not great. Don't listen to them, Padma."

Meanwhile, Lizzy sat scribbling in her notebook. She looked up and said, "Guys, I'm trying to think here."

"Why start now?" Connor joked.

"Funny," Lizzy said, scrunching her nose. "I still don't know why I'm the one who has to give the speech."

"Because we elected you," Connor said.

"Elected me? When did that happen?" Lizzy asked.

Connor looked from Deon to Kym to Padma. "Everybody who thinks Lizzy should be the one to give the big speech, raise your hand."

Five hands shot to the ceiling. (Deon raised both.)

Lizzy groaned. "I don't even know what to say."

"You'll think of something," Connor said.

Lizzy wasn't so sure.

"Just stand up and tell everybody what's what," Deon said.

"Sure, okay, I'll just, you know—" Lizzy paused, looking to her friends for help. "And I'll say that—and then, um . . ."

"Her ears are twitching," Connor noticed.

Padma giggled.

Lizzy's cheeks flushed red. She banged her hand on the table. Markers jumped in the air. "I'm telling you. I can't do it."

"Sure you can," Connor said.

"You'll be great," Kym added.

Lizzy put on a brave face.

But deep down, she was terrified.

— CHAPTER 10 —

Lizzy Gets a Little Help

It was decided.

Lizzy was the best choice. Everyone knew it. Even Lizzy herself. This idea had started with her. She had to be the one to stand before the entire school.

Whether she liked it or not.

On Wednesday, one day before the presentations, Miss Zips checked in with the gang. They were huddled on the rug, including Padma.

"Are you all set with your speech for tomorrow?" Miss Zips asked.

"It's really good," Kym said. She smiled in Lizzy's direction.

Lizzy swallowed, unconvinced.

Miss Zips sat down on the rug, her long legs folding like a lawn chair. She said to Lizzy, "You have your claim—your big idea, right?"

Lizzy nodded.

"And you've done your research to support that claim?" She looked to the others for encouragement.

"Oh yes," Kym said.

"Padma had a great idea," Deon said. "We can

use her art to make a new dragon logo for the school. We can probably sell T-shirts and coffee mugs and other stuff."

"We can raise money for charity," Padma said.

"I like that very much," Miss Zips said. "That should be very appealing to the rest of the school. Don't you think, Lizzy?"

Lizzy nodded again. But she stayed quiet. She was like an empty home. People could ring and ring, but she wouldn't answer the door.

"It's important to hook the listeners right away," Miss Zips reminded Lizzy. "Do you have an attention grabber?"

Lizzy sat perfectly still. Eyes downcast, she shook her head once. In truth, Lizzy felt dizzy in her stomach. As if a hundred caterpillars, with their ticklish toes, crawled around inside her belly. It was her job to persuade the entire school. Just thinking about it made her want to hurl.

"She'll do great!" Deon said.

He clapped Lizzy on the back.

"Yeah," Kym agreed.

Everyone brimmed with hope. But Lizzy remained silent. Her speech was almost ready. She had a big idea. She had three main reasons, supported by facts. And she had a strong ending. But Lizzy was missing one thing. She didn't have a snazzy opener.

And time was slipping away.

On the way to lunch, students paused outside the cafeteria. Connor stared at yet another armadillo poster, frowning. "I just don't get it. Padma's dragon is so much cooler."

"What's to get?" Lizzy snapped. "Some people love armadillos."

"Seriously?" Connor asked.

"Well, obviously!" Lizzy barked.

Lizzy nudged past her brother, pushed past everyone. She clomped into the cafeteria as if she had an important meeting with a cardboard tray of spaghetti and meatballs.

"What's with your sister?" Deon asked.

"She gets like this when she's nervous," Connor replied.

"No worries," Deon said. "She'll knock it out of the park."

"I guess," Connor said. He folded his arms across his soccer jersey. Connor didn't seem convinced.

Neither was Lizzy.

She was scared.

Lizzy thought and thought. But no ideas came. Her speech needed something extra. How was she going to rally the students behind Drake the Dragon?

During lunch, Connor left his seat with the boys. He sat beside his sister. "You okay?" he asked.

Lizzy looked up at her twin, surprised. She lifted her shoulders and let them drop. A shrug.

"I feel like I might throw up," she confessed.

"Not a good idea," Connor said. "But if you do, find a garbage can. Learn from my mistakes."

Lizzy smiled. "Yeah, thanks."

"I was thinking about how you said you need a catchy beginning," Connor said.

"An attention grabber," Lizzy said. "Do you have one?"

"Um, not a clue." Connor grinned. He paused, then asked, "Do you remember how Miss Zips said ideas are like seeds?"

Yes, Lizzy nodded.

Connor said, "Seeds need water, light, and soil to grow. But ideas are different. They need hard work and time. Your idea will come. Just give it time."

Lizzy shook her head. "That's the problem, Connor. I'm running out of time."

Connor placed a hand on his sister's shoulder. "Don't tell anyone, Lizzy, but you're my best friend in the world. And I'm here to say, I know you've got this."

Lizzy looked down. Something in her heart stirred. Her mood lightened. Lizzy slid over a plastic container of three small chocolate chip cookies. "You can have them. I'm full."

To Connor, it was better than a hug.

Lizzy thought, maybe ideas really were like seeds. Yes, they needed hard work and time. But maybe, Lizzy decided, ideas needed friendship, too.

Maybe friendship was the soil.

She was happy to share her cookies with Connor.

And in that moment, as her wild twin scarfed down his third cookie, the idea came.

— CHAPTER 11 —

Imagine

The entire school squeezed into the cafetorium. That's what they called the cafeteria after lunch. It was basically an auditorium that smelled bad. The floor had been swept, the tables cleared away.

All the students, K through five, sat on the floor. Lizzy waited by a side entrance, as instructed. Connor, Deon, and Kym waited with her. Partly to show their support. Partly because they were worried she might flee the building.

A fifth-grade teacher, Mr. Alvarez, poked his head into the hallway. "Are you all set, Lizzy? We should be ready to begin in just another minute."

Lizzy gulped and checked the index cards in her hand, and her ears twitched.

"Don't worry," Kym said.

"You'll do great," Deon said.

"And don't hurl," Connor joked.

"You're gross," Kym said. "Has anyone ever told you that?"

"Yeah, a few times," Connor said, smiling. He didn't seem to mind.

Lizzy shook her head, laughing.

Mr. Alvarez nodded to Lizzy, and she took her seat on the stage beside Suri. Principal Tux-

bury walked to the podium. He made a few opening remarks. He called Suri forward. As Suri stood up, Lizzy leaned over to squeeze her hand. "Good luck," Lizzy said.

Suri smiled. "Thanks, that's sweet. You too."

Suri spoke in a calm, clear voice. She seemed a little jittery, but not too bad. Suri spoke about affection for Arnold, how unique an armadillo mascot is, and the importance of tradition. The students applauded enthusiastically.

Now it was Lizzy's turn.

Lizzy cleared her throat.

She looked out into the sea of faces, the way Miss Zips had told her to.

Seconds crawled past.

"You can start anytime," Principal Tuxbury whispered. "We're all ears."

Lizzy leaned into the microphone. It buzzed. She tried again.

"Close your eyes," she said in a soft voice.

The audience shifted on the floor, uncertain. Until one by one, they sat in silence, eyes shut.

Waiting.

Lizzy said, "Now remember all the happy days you've spent as a kid, watching armadillos play outside your window."

Lizzy paused.

One set of eyes opened. Then another.

"You don't remember, do you?" Lizzy said. "Me neither."

Lizzy forced a laugh from her throat. "The truth is, there aren't any armadillos in Connecticut. Never were."

Some of the kids laughed. Others just smiled. It didn't matter. From that moment on, Lizzy had them in the palm of her hand.

"Suri is right. Arnold has been a good mascot for Clay Elementary," Lizzy said. "He's been around for a long time. For years and years and years." Lizzy allowed her voice to drag here, sounding tired. Then she brightened. "But now we have a chance for something fresh, something new."

Lizzy looked out into the audience. "Tradition is nice. But things change. We can't let tradition keep us from getting better. Tradition can become a trap. We become chained to old ideas."

"Here's another tradition to consider—the tradition of change. We've done our research. Many schools and even professional teams have changed their mascots over the years. For example, the Adams State Grizzlies used to be the Indians. At Arizona State, they went from the Owls to the Bulldogs to the Sun Devils. Right here in Connecticut, we love our Huskies. But did you know they used to be called the States-men?"

A few snickers filled the room. Lizzy raised a hand. "There are hundreds of hilarious examples. Everyone knows Mr. Met, the famous mascot for the New York Mets. But not many people remember that they once had a mule for a mascot. A mule named Mettle." Lizzy smiled at the audience. "It was a really, really bad idea."

"It is our school, our vote, our voice. It should be our idea. With your vote today, we can start our own tradition at Clay Elementary. We can make our own mark on the future."

Lizzy told the gathered students about Padma's idea for raising money. "Drake the Dragon will create new excitement. We'll sell T-shirts and banners. We'll raise money—and we'll use that money to improve our amazing school."

This earned a big roar from the audience.

"What's more," Lizzy said, her voice strong and confident, "let's get real. Let's be honest here. Dragons are fierce. Dragons are magical.

Dragons are cool. Imagine a battle between an armadillo and a dragon. Seriously? I don't have to tell you who would win that one."

She paused, leaned into the microphone, and whispered, "Roasted, toasted armadillo. Every time."

More laughter filled the room.

"One last thing before we all vote," Lizzy said. "My parents always told me to be myself. 'Lizzy, be yourself,' they'd say. But then my father would add with a wink, 'Unless you can be a dragon. Then always be a dragon.'"

Lizzy caught Connor's eye in the crowd. He nodded, a big grin on his face.

"Let's do it, Clay Elementary," Lizzy said. "Let's all be Dragons together!"

The room went wild. Connor, Kym, and Deon leaped to their feet, shouting and cheering.

Lizzy should have felt thrilled. But mostly, after it was over, she just felt . . . glad it was over. Relieved she didn't hurl in front of the entire school.

The only thing left was the vote.

And the waiting.

The winner would be announced at the end of the day.

Miss Zips surprised the class with a small party of cookies, brownies, and drinks. "Today has been a great day for Clay Elementary," Miss Zips said. "It doesn't matter which side wins. The important thing is that you all voted. I hope you liked that feeling. It's a privilege. And I hope you vote many, many times in the future."

The class cheered.

Bobby Mumford spilled a cup of juice.

Because of course he did. That's how Bobby rolled. Mr. Sanders hustled to help clean up the mess with paper towels. "No worries, good thing it's not on the rug," he said cheerfully.

Bobby smiled and filled a new cup.

"You did good today," Suri said to Lizzy. "I thought your speech was really great."

"Thanks," Lizzy said. "So was yours."

"I was really nervous," Suri confessed.

"Huh? It didn't look that way," Lizzy said. "You looked large and in charge."

Suri smiled. "Yes, sure, for someone who wanted to throw up!"

Lizzy laughed. "You too? I guess we both felt that way."

Then a voice came from the loudspeaker. "Good afternoon, Clay Elementary!" Principal Tuxbury announced.

"I'm sure you are all eager to learn the results of today's vote," he said. "But first, let's give one more cheer for our two outstanding candidates—Arnold the Armadillo and Drake the Dragon!"

Whoops and shouts echoed throughout the building.

"Arnold received a total of one hundred and eighty-three votes," Principal Tuxbury said. "But the winner this year, with three hundred and forty-seven votes, is Drake the Dragon! It looks like Clay Elementary will have a new mascot!"

— CHAPTER 12 —

Enter the Dragon

A month later, there was a surprise assembly in the school cafetorium.

"What's this about?" the class asked Miss Zips.

"You'll see," she said.

When everyone was seated on the floor, the lights were turned down. Miss Zips stepped onto the stage. She spoke into a microphone. "As you remember, we all had a big vote last month on the school mascot."

The audience cheered.

"Today we are officially the Clay Elementary Dragons!"

The cheers grew into a roar.

"We'd like to celebrate today with a little surprise." She held up a finger. "But first, some business. We used the beautiful artwork created by Padma Bitar for the design of new T-shirts. Sales have already been a huge success. Thank you all for supporting your school."

Miss Zips pumped both fists into the air. The crowd went bananas. It took a minute for everyone to quiet down. "Good ideas don't fall from the sky. They come from real people who put in time and energy to make things happen."

At this point, Miss Zips read the names of five students to stand up on stage with her: Lizzy O'Malley, Connor O'Malley, Kym Park, Deon Gibson, and Padma Bitar.

Hoots and shouts greeted them. "Hi, Deon!" A girl swooned.

Finally, Miss Zips announced, "And now for our special surprise."

The curtain opened. Suddenly a dragon with red wings flew across the stage. Well, actually, it was someone in the costume of a dragon. The wings were just arms with extra red material.

"Way to go, Principal Tuxbury!" a voice called out. The kids stomped their feet on the floor, creating a thunderous roar.

"Way cooler than an armadillo," Connor whispered to Lizzy.

Kym turned around. "Maybe we should've gone with the hamster," she said.

Then she laughed. "Not really!"

Miss Zips's "Wow Me" Tips

Have you ever tried to convince your parents to let you stay up late? Perhaps you want to get a family pet, or take a trip to Disney World? Have you ever tried to get out of cleaning your room or doing your homework? If so, you've been practicing your persuasion skills!

You've probably noticed that whining and begging are not the most effective ways to persuade somebody. Making a logical argument is a much better way to get others to see your point of view, because you are giving them reasons to be persuaded. Let's start at the beginning.

What's the big idea?

Presenting an argument is not about being the loudest, or the funniest, or even the smartest. As

I tell my students all the time, it's about making a claim, and supporting that claim with evidence.

What do you need to convince your audience of? A claim often starts with a big idea. An idea is "big" if it is something you feel excited or passionate about. If you don't feel strongly, how can you convince anyone else to agree with you?

Lizzy and Kym had the big idea that their school should get a new mascot. To turn that idea into a claim, the BIG needed to be specific, direct, and make one main point: Drake the Dragon would make a better mascot for Clay Elementary than Arnold the Armadillo. There is no question about what they are arguing!

Now what? Support that claim!

Supporting your claim means trying to prove it. Think about it this way: if you simply made a claim and stopped there, your audience would be left wondering, WHY? So you have to answer that question for them. You have to give your audience reasons to be persuaded, and back those reasons up with evidence such as facts and details.

It's always good to start by asking yourself some questions. For example:

- **Why isn't the armadillo a good mascot?**

- **Why would a dragon make a better mascot?**

- **Why might anyone want to keep the armadillo mascot, and how can I argue against that?**

- **What are the benefits of getting a new mascot?**

Being able to answer these kinds of "why" questions will give you the reasons for your argument and help you come up with the facts and details you need to support your claim.

Let's look at Lizzy's speech. What support

does she offer to convince Clay Elementary to vote for a dragon mascot?

REASON: An armadillo doesn't make sense as a mascot for an elementary school in Connecticut.

EVIDENCE: They are warm-weather animals and there are no armadillos living in Connecticut or anywhere close.

REASON: A new mascot could help raise money to improve the school.

EVIDENCE: The new dragon image could help sell T-shirts, banners, etc.

REASON: Dragons could take down any opponent!

EVIDENCE: They are magical and fierce.

Now that you've made your claim and supported it with reasons and evidence, it's time to wrap everything up in the conclusion of your argument. This is your last chance to get your audience to agree with your point of view—make the most of it! In your conclusion, you can restate your claim, tie up any loose ends, and make a call to action if needed. A call to action asks your audience to believe something or do something. In Lizzy's speech, she says, "Let's all be Dragons together!" This is a call to action because she is asking the other students to vote for Drake the Dragon.

Put it all together!

What we've just gone over are the basic elements of a strong argument. This is a good format to follow for your next persuasive speech or writing assignment:

CLAIM

Reason
Evidence
Reason
Evidence
Reason
Evidence

CONCLUSION

So, what's *your* big idea? Better get to work—you've got a lot of convincing to do, and I want you to wow me!